This book belongs to

_____

Published by Advance Publishers
© 1998 Disney Enterprises, Inc.
All rights reserved. Printed in the United States.
No part of this book may be reproduced or copied in any form
without the written permission of the copyright owner.

Written by Ronald Kidd
Illustrated by Peter Emslie and Eric Binder
Produced by Bumpy Slide Books

ISBN: 1-57973-007-8

10 9 8 7 6 5 4 3 2

When Hercules was a young man, he longed to go live on Mount Olympus with his father, Zeus. But getting there wouldn't be easy. First he would have to prove himself a true hero, and that would take more than just strength. To teach Hercules all about it, Zeus sent him to see Philoctetes, the trainer of heroes.

Phil looked the boy up and down. "A true hero, huh? You know, it's not the sort of thing you learn in one day, even if Zeus is your dad. Takes years of practice, and even then, who knows?"

"Just tell me what to do," said Hercules. "I'm going to be the best student you've ever had!"

Phil handed him a bow and arrow. "Okay, kid, can you hit the bull's-eye on that target?"

"No problem," said Hercules. He drew back the arrow until the bow was bent nearly double. Then he let the arrow go.

The arrow sped through the air — over the target, across the field, and into a tree. It landed with such force that the tree was ripped from the ground. The tree fell against another tree, knocking that tree down, which fell into another. On and on the trees toppled, like a row of dominoes.

Phil stared at the trees. "Kid, you are something else. Unfortunately, whatever that something is, it's got nothing to do with archery."

"Tell you what," said the trainer, handing him a discus. "As long as you're going for distance, how about giving this a whirl?"

Taking the discus, Hercules began spinning around, faster and faster, like a human tornado.

The wind rose, and dark clouds gathered overhead. Just when it seemed he could spin no faster, Hercules let go of the discus. It rocketed into the sky and pierced the clouds, causing a torrential downpour.

"Did I mention that I hate rain?" said Phil, dripping wet.

"Okay, forget about throwing things," said
the trainer. "Let's rescue a damsel in distress."
He pointed to an abandoned hut nearby.

"Picture this, kid. Inside that building is a beautiful girl who needs to be saved. Can you do it?"

"Just watch me!" said Hercules.

Hercules rammed into the building, smashing
a giant hole in the wall. The building collapsed into
a heap of stones.

"Nice, very nice," Phil said, "except remember
the damsel inside? She's flat as pita bread."

Hercules sighed. "It's no use, Phil. I'll never be a true hero."

"Sure you will," said the trainer. "You just need practice, that's all — lots of practice. Oh, and one more thing: Always remember that, no matter how strong you are, there's something else that's more important."

"What's that?" asked Hercules.

Phil yelled, "Think, kid! You have to think!"

And so Hercules began his training. Every day he practiced what Phil had taught him. But as hard as he tried, he kept messing things up. It seemed that he couldn't do anything right.

By the end of the first week Hercules was ready for a break, so he climbed onto Pegasus and flew off into the sky for some much-needed rest and relaxation.

As they were happily swooping through the air, weaving around the clouds, they didn't notice that the sky had grown darker. Before they knew it, they were in the middle of a thunderstorm, with lightning bolts flashing all around them.

Hercules guessed that these lightning bolts were being hurled from the top of Mount Olympus by his father, Zeus. Determined to know that same feeling of power, Hercules flew after a stray lightning bolt, then reached out and caught it in his hand.

Hercules zoomed back to Earth, clutching the lightning bolt and pretending to aim it at statues, chariots, and houses.

"Zap!" he said as he whizzed by. "You're ancient history!"

Soon he grew tired of pretending. Besides, he was proud to have the lightning bolt and wanted to show someone. So he went off in search of Philoctetes.

Hercules found him at home, reading.

"Hey, Phil, look what I've got!" he exclaimed.

"Go away, kid. It's Saturday," replied the old trainer, his nose buried in the morning scroll.

Grinning mischievously, Hercules gathered some sticks into a pile and aimed the lightning bolt. Zap! The sticks burst into flame!

"Hey!" cried Phil. "Doesn't that hot new toy belong to your ol' man?"

"That's right," said Hercules, "and when I get to Mount Olympus, I'll have as many of these as I want."

"That's fine, kid," said Phil, "but just watch what you're doing. And remember — think, always think! That lightning bolt might be more complicated than it looks."

"Nah, it's simple," Hercules said. "Just point and shoot."

Shrugging, Phil said, "So what's with the campfire? You planning a wienie roast?"

"How about a fish fry instead?" answered Hercules. He netted some fish and roasted them, then settled down by the fire with his trainer for a tasty lunch.

After they finished, Hercules had another idea. "Hey, how about we test this lightning bolt out at the rock quarry?"

"What are you, crazy?" said Phil. "That thing can't blast through rock!"

Hercules grinned. "We'll see," he replied.

Leaving Pegasus behind, they descended into
the quarry. When they came to a stack of boulders,
Hercules pointed the lightning bolt.

Zap! The boulders exploded in a thousand pieces.
As they continued down the path, Hercules
pointed the lightning bolt again and again. Zap! Zap!

Zap! Zap! Zap!
   "Be careful with that thing!" Phil said.
   "Relax," said Hercules. "Any idiot can use it."
   Phil nodded. "That's what I'm afraid of."

Hercules blasted his way out of the rock quarry, and a short time later they found themselves in the forest. They followed a narrow trail that curved through the trees. But Hercules was growing impatient.

"Stand back, Phil," he said. "I'm going to widen this path."

Before the old trainer could say anything,
Hercules had pointed the lightning bolt. Zap!
    Just as he had hoped, a wide path appeared
among the trees. But something else appeared,
too — flames. Hercules had set the forest on fire!

On Mount Olympus, Zeus was just putting away his lightning bolts when he smelled something in the air. He looked down from the clouds and saw a plume of smoke rising from the forest below.

"Fire!" cried Zeus. He immediately grabbed a storm cloud and squeezed it until he'd made a downpour. Luckily, the rain put out the flames in no time flat.

At Phil's insistence, Hercules traveled to the Temple of Zeus to apologize for what he had done. The statue came to life, and Zeus took back the lightning bolt from Hercules.

"Remember," he instructed his son, "being a true hero takes more than just strength and power."

The next morning, as Hercules went for a ride on Pegasus, a winged figure sped into view. It was Hermes, the messenger.

"Bad news!" said Hermes. "An army has surrounded Corinth, and they're about to attack!"

Hercules flew to Phil's side and asked, "What can we do to stop them?"

"I don't know," Phil replied, "but I'll tell you one thing: We sure could use that lightning bolt."

Hercules said, "It's my fault that we don't have it.

And now I'm going to make up for it. After all, I'm in training to be a hero, aren't I?" He leapt onto Pegasus and raced off.

Phil called after him, "Wait, kid! Don't leave! You're not ready yet!"

But Hercules was already gone.

Landing on a mountaintop in Corinth, Hercules used his amazing strength to start an avalanche big enough to head off the invading army. As he watched, though, the boulders he had thrown veered away from the soldiers and into the city.

Without meaning to, Hercules had helped the invaders!

Luckily the people of Corinth saw the boulders coming and were able to escape. But the army was still charging toward them.

Hercules wasn't ready to give up. He called to the people of Corinth, "Don't worry, I'll save you!"

The people shouted back, "No, don't! Please, go save someone else!"

But Hercules wouldn't listen. He leapt onto Pegasus and winged his way to a river near the city. Using his bare hands, he built a dam to block the river and send its waters flowing toward the soldiers.

Unfortunately, it flowed right past them and flooded the city! Once again, Hercules had helped the wrong side.

The people were able to escape the flood by moving to a hill, but it made them a perfect target for the invaders. Hercules looked on in horror as the army closed in.

Philoctetes joined him a moment later. "Didn't go so well, huh, kid?"

Hercules shook his head sadly. "You were right, Phil. I'm not ready to be a hero. The more I try to help these people, the more I hurt them."

"It may not be too late," the old trainer said. "Remember, kid — think! You've got to think!"

So that's what Hercules did. He thought. And he thought. And suddenly, he knew what he must do.

Hercules approached the leader of the invaders and whispered something in the man's ear.

The leader stared at him, terrified, and turned to his troops. "Retreat!" he shouted. "Let's get out of here!"

Phil looked on, stunned, as the invaders turned and headed off over the horizon.

"You were right, Phil," said Hercules, landing nearby. "It takes more than strength to be a hero. So I tried thinking, and I figured it out."

"What?" said Phil. "What did you tell the guy?"

Hercules grinned. "I told him the one thing he didn't want to hear. I told him that now I was going to help him just like I helped the people of Corinth!"

In the weeks that followed, Hercules practiced and finally learned how to use his strength. But he never forgot the lesson he learned that day at Corinth: When it comes to being a hero, a whisper can be as loud as a lightning bolt.

Hercules had strength to spare,
But that was not enough.
It takes lots more than muscles
To succeed when life gets tough.
Phil taught his boy that brains
Are what you need
To do what's right —
So always think,
And think some more
Before you use your might!